Published by Ladybird Books Ltd
80 Strand London WC2R 0RL
A Penguin Company
9 10 8

© Jean and Gareth Adamson MCMXCVII

Printed in China

# Topsy + Tim

## Busy Builders

Jean and Gareth Adamson

When Topsy and Tim looked out of the window for the first time on Tuesday morning, they saw a big digger parked at the end of the garden next door.

Mr Fen, who lived next door, came out of his house and said, "Hello," to the man on the digger. Topsy and Tim ran out into their garden and said, "Hello!" too.

"This is my friend, Eric," called
Mr Fen to Topsy and Tim. "Eric and
his helpers are builders. They're
going to build a garage for me, here
at the end of my garden."

"What's the digger for?" asked Tim.
"That's to dig the foundations of
the garage," said Eric.

"Come along, Topsy and Tim,"
called Mummy from the kitchen.
"Time to go to playgroup."

After playgroup, Topsy and Tim hurried home as fast as possible. They couldn't wait to see how the builders were getting on.

The digger had already dug a large,
neat, square hole at the end of
Mr Fen's garden.

When Eric saw Topsy and Tim
he called to them, "Hello, twins!
Do you think your mum would give
us some hot water to make our
coffee?"

Topsy and Tim each carried one of the builders' flasks. Each flask had some milk and coffee powder in the bottom.

Mummy poured hot water into
the flasks, and they were full of
steaming coffee.

Topsy and Tim wanted to help
Mummy take the coffee out to the
builders, but Eric came to the back
door to fetch it.

"Come on, twins," he said. "Come
and meet my mates."

Eric's helpers were sitting on a long plank, eating sandwiches and cake. Their names were Joe and Jim. They were pleased to meet Topsy and Tim.

"Have you ever had a ride in a wheelbarrow?" asked Eric.

He gave Topsy and Tim hard-hats to wear, and he put a clean sack in the bottom of the wheelbarrow.

Then he gave them wonderful rides
round and round Mr Fen's garden.

"Time for lunch," called Mummy,
over the garden fence.

While they ate their lunch, Topsy and Tim watched the builders through the kitchen window. They waved to them again and again.

Joe and Jim weren't always looking,
but Eric waved back every time.

After lunch Eric called to them,
"I need two strong workers to help
me shovel some sand!"

Mummy found their seaside spades.

"I'm taking bigger spadefuls!"
said Tim.

"I'm digging faster than you!"
said Topsy.

"You're *both* doing very well!"
said Eric.

At four o'clock Mummy brought them some apple juice in their own flasks, and they ate their sandwiches sitting on the builders' long plank… because Topsy and Tim were busy builders, too!

Put the pictures in order and tell the story.

# Match each one to its home.

Point to the things that begin with the same sound as 'busy' and 'builder'.

Look at the picture.

How many wheelbarrows can
you count?
How many cement mixers?
How many yellow hats?
How many blue hats?